#5 Crane Fly Crash

Books in the
S.W.I.T.C.H. series

S.W.I.T.C.H.

#5 Crane Fly Crash

Ali Sparkes

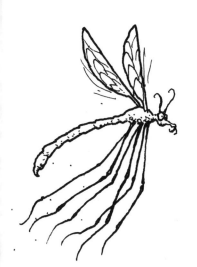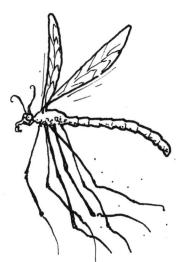

illustrated by
Ross Collins

darbycreek

MINNEAPOLIS

Text © Ali Sparkes 2011
Illustrations © Ross Collins 2011

"SWITCH: Crane Fly Crash" was originally published in English in 2011. This edition is published by an arrangement with Oxford University Press.

Darby Creek
A division of Lerner Publishing Group, Inc.
241 First Avenue North
Minneapolis, MN 55401 U.S.A.

Website address: www.lernerbooks.com

Main body text set in ITC Goudy Sans Std. 14/19.
Typeface provided by Monotype Typography.

Library of Congress Cataloging-in-Publication Data

Sparkes, Ali.
        Crane fly crash / by Ali Sparkes ; illustrated by Ross Collins.
            p.   cm. — (S.W.I.T.C.H. ; #05)
        Summary: When their sister, Jenny, is accidentally turned into a crane fly by Petty Potts' SWITCH spray, twins Josh and Danny must transform themselves, as well, and rescue her before she burns her legs off.
        ISBN 978-0-7613-9203-3 (lib. bdg. : alk. paper)
        [1. Flies—Fiction. 2. Brothers and sisters—Fiction. 3. Twins—Fiction. 4. Science fiction.] I. Collins, Ross, ill. II. Title.
        PZ7.S73712Cr 2013
        [Fic]—dc23   2012026636

Manufactured in the United States of America
1 – SB – 12/31/12

For Freddie Michael

Danny and Josh
(and Piddle)

They may be twins, but they're NOT the same! Josh loves insects, spiders, beetles, and bugs. Danny can't stand them. Anything little with multiple legs freaks him out. So sharing a bedroom with Josh can be ... erm ... interesting. Mind you, they both love putting earwigs in big sister Jenny's underwear drawer ...

Danny

- FULL NAME: Danny Phillips
- AGE: eight years
- HEIGHT: taller than Josh
- FAVORITE THING: skateboarding
- WORST THING: creepy-crawlies and cleaning
- AMBITION: to be a stuntman

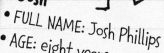

Josh
- FULL NAME: Josh Phillips
- AGE: eight years
- HEIGHT: taller than Danny
- FAVORITE THING: collecting insects
- WORST THING: skateboarding
- AMBITION: to be an entomologist

Piddle
- FULL NAME: Piddle the dog Phillips
- AGE: two dog years (fourteen in human years)
- HEIGHT: not very
- FAVORITE THING: chasing sticks
- WORST THING: cats
- AMBITION: to bite a squirrel

Contents

Something in the Hair Tonight

A horrific murder was about to take place in a dark alley. The victim fluttered helplessly in the shadow of a terrifying spiked weapon that pounded against the wall. It missed only by inches.

The murderer was cold. Unfeeling. Able to kill with a single blow and then turn away without a moment's remorse. The victim knew time was nearly up. One more attack and there would be nothing left but a mashed corpse.

The spiked weapon swung forward.

"Jenny! Stop it!" Josh leaped across his big sister's bedroom floor. He grabbed her arm just before it swung the hairbrush down again.

"Hey! Get off!" yelled Jenny, trying to shake her little brother off her arm. But now his twin,

Danny, came running in too. With an excited whoop he threw himself at her other arm.

"You're a murderer!" shrieked Josh. "Killing innocent moths! How could you?"

The poor moth in question flapped limply up the wall from behind Jenny's bed and bumbled against the windowpane, trying to get away.

"It's just a *moth*, Josh! Not a cat or a dog or a person!" snapped Jenny. Her long blonde hair whipped about as she wrestled with her brothers.

"Just because it's small, doesn't mean it doesn't have feelings," said Danny. He climbed onto his sister's back and made her spin round furiously.

"Danny! *Get off!*" Jenny whacked her elbows back. Danny fell onto her bed. Josh had let his sister go. He was now peering closely at the brown moth. Jenny shook her head at Danny. "You don't even *like* creepy-crawlies. You go nuts if one lands on *you*!"

"True," shrugged Danny. "They can be creepy. But they are quite amazing too. I should know. I've been a spider, you know. And a bluebottle. And a grasshopper. Oh—and an ant. That was amazing!"

"Yeah, right," snorted Jenny. "Well, you always creep *me* out, anyway!"

Danny laughed. He knew Jenny couldn't possibly believe what he'd just said. Even though it was true. He and Josh *had* been all those creatures over the summer. Ever since they stumbled into the secret laboratory in their neighbor's garden, they had discovered something incredible.

Their neighbor, Petty Potts, might seem like a batty old lady, but it turned out she was a genius scientist. She had invented S.W.I.T.C.H., a spray that could turn you into a creepy-crawly. Only Danny and Josh knew her secret since the day when they had accidentally got sprayed and turned into spiders. They'd been afraid of her at first. But now they were helping her by searching for some special missing cubes. They'd got four already. If they found just two more, Petty would have the code to make a new S.W.I.T.C.H. spray, which could change you into a reptile. They could find out how it felt to be snake or a lizard or even an alligator!

"You don't *have* to kill him, you know," Josh told Jenny, still examining the moth. "All you have to do is open the window."

"I've tried that," huffed Jenny. "But it just keeps flying back in!"

"You need to turn your light off," explained

Josh. He reached over and switched off Jenny's bedside lamp. "Moths get confused and think it's the moon. They keep flying toward it." He eased open the window, blew gently on the moth, and smiled as it flew away into the night. "Off you go, hawky!" he called after it. "Go get your tea!" He closed the window and glanced back into the room. Danny was squirming on the bed with Jenny's foot on his head. "It's a hawk moth. They feed on nectar by moonlight. Isn't that sweet? And they can smell their girlfriends from miles and miles away."

"Ugh," commented Danny.

"Yeah, thanks for the biology lesson, you freaky little bug geek," said Jenny. She released Danny and switched her lamp back on. "Now get out of my room, both of you. I've got to get ready to go out." And she flounced to her mirror and started to brush her hair with the deadly weapon. She rummaged through all the bottles and pots of hair and makeup stuff. "MOM!" she bellowed, ignoring them. "Where's my hair spray?"

Mom didn't answer. She was singing along to the radio in the kitchen. The doorbell rang as Josh and Danny mooched out of Jenny's room. They shrugged at each other. Jenny was such a teenager.

Danny slid down the banister. He leaped off at the bottom step, landing with a thud by the front door and opening it a second later.

Standing on the doorstep was Petty Potts. As soon as she saw Danny and Josh stepping up behind him, she darted her eyes left and right behind her thick glasses. She hissed, "Excellent! The very people I was hoping for!" Her tweedy old hat was pulled down low over her face. The collar of her old trench coat was turned up. She looked as if she was pretending to be a spy.

"Shhhhhh!" said Petty, not coming into the house but leaning closer to them. "Now listen. This is very important. Very important."

"What is?" said Danny.

"Hush! Shhhh!" Petty pulled her coat tight across her chest and frowned at Danny. "I need your help. But only you two must know!"

Josh sighed. Sometimes he thought Petty didn't even realize that she was a senior citizen and he and Danny were still in elementary school. She behaved as if they were all the same age. "What is it, Petty?" he asked, warily.

Whenever they got involved with Petty Potts, they always seemed to end up uncomfortably close to being dead.

Petty glanced around again. "I am going away to a conference in Berlin," she said, in a low voice. "A very important conference."

"Are you going to show off your S.W.I.T.C.H. spray?" asked Danny.

"No! No! Not yet." Petty looked quite alarmed. "The world of science is not ready. I can't reveal my secrets now! Not yet. But—if something were to happen to me . . ." She peered at them, slowly nodding her head. "Oh yes—something *could* happen to me. Then my work might never ever be known! And that—*that*—would be a tragedy!"

"Do you think someone's after you then?" whispered Josh.

Petty squinted at him. "What?"

"You know," said Josh. "I mean—you've said before that you think people are spying on you. But do you think they're actually out to get you? Like in movies?"

"Good grief, no," said Petty, as if she thought Josh was simple-minded. "I just mean that I might get run over by a bus or something. And of course, that could happen at any time! Anyway, just in case it does, while I am away, I want you to keep this!" And she pulled a plastic spray bottle out of her coat, the kind with a squirty button on the top and a little plastic cap over the button.

"We don't want that!" gasped Danny, backing away.

"Oh for heaven's sake! It's perfectly safe—all sealed tight," said Petty. "Just pop it under your bed or something and keep it until I get back. Then if I *don't* come back for any reason, you can take it to *New Scientist* magazine and reveal my genius to the world."

"Petty," said Josh, "have you ever noticed that we're not grown-ups? I mean . . . you do realize that we're only eight, don't you?"

"What's that got to do with anything?" said Petty, thrusting the bottle into Josh's hands. She turned and walked back down the path. "See you next week, all being well! Take care, now. And keep searching for the cubes!"

Josh and Danny closed the door and stared at the bottle. "Wonder which type of spray it is," muttered Danny. "Maybe . . . bee or wasp. Or centipede . . ."

"We are not going to find out," said Josh.

Danny nodded. Their creepy-crawly adventures had been exciting. But they had both been nearly eaten far too many times now to want to take a chance with Petty's latest spray.

It was still hard to believe, but Petty Potts had created S.W.I.T.C.H. spray in the underground lab in her garden. She used a secret formula she had worked out during her years with the government in a top-secret science department. She might be there still if her so-called friend, the eyebrow-less Victor Crouch, had not tried to steal her work and then wipe out her memory.

His plan was foiled, though, because Petty had suspected foul play. She had put a fake formula in her work desk and hidden the *real* secret S.W.I.T.C.H. formula inside six little glass cubes.

Then she had re-created it at home when bits of
her memory began to come back. It really worked.
Josh and Danny ought to know. They'd been
S.W.I.T.C.H.ed four times now.

"Come on," said Josh, heading up the stairs.
"Let's take this up to our room and find a
place to hide it. She's better off not having it,
probably. She sprays way too much of this stuff
around."

"We really should just try to stay away from her! Not answer the door next time," said Danny.

"I know," said Josh. "But . . . if we ever *did* find all her other lost secret formula cubes . . . well . . . " He bit his lip, but his eyes shone. Petty had made a second secret formula. It was to create a spray that could switch them into reptiles. She put it into another six cubes. Only she'd lost them. So far they'd only found four. Without the last two, it could never work.

"Imagine," continued Josh. "I could be a snake!"

"I could be an alligator!" said Danny.

"*If* we ever find the last two REPTOSWITCH cubes . . . " sighed Josh. Petty had begged them both to search for her. But who knew where the missing cubes could be? The first four they'd found around the yards and houses in their neighborhood. But they might never find the last two. Petty had hidden them too well. That bit of her memory—about where they were—had not come back.

"I could be a giant tree lizard . . ." went on Danny.

Suddenly something swung down from the top of the banister. "Hey! You little monsters! I knew you'd been messing with my stuff! Gimme my hair spray now!" And Jenny swiped the bottle out of Josh's hands before he could even squeak.

"HEY NO! NO! JENNY, THAT'S NOT YOURS!" shouted Josh. In reply, Jenny just slammed her bedroom door. Josh and Danny stood on the stairs and stared at each other in horror. Then they hurtled up to the landing and across to Jenny's room.

"JENNY! DON'T USE THAT! DON'T SPRAY IT!" they shrieked, in utter panic, crashing her door wide open.

"OUT of my room!" shouted Jenny. She had taken the plastic cap off the spray bottle. She was holding it up to her swept-back hair.

"Jenny! Please!" begged Josh, feeling his head reel with panic. "DO NOT USE THAT SPRAY! It's not what you think it is!"

"Oh ha-ha!" said Jenny. "Very funny." And she sprayed a huge cloud of S.W.I.T.C.H. spray all over her head.

Fishcakes on Roller Skates

"What are you staring at?" demanded Jenny,
slamming the S.W.I.T.C.H. spray onto her dressing
table as the pale yellow mist settled on her hair
and shoulders. "Get out of my r—"

And then she disappeared.

Danny and Josh stood very still. They didn't dare
move. Jenny could be *anything*. And she could be
anywhere! If she was a fly or an ant, she could be
right where they might tread if they moved.

"Can you see anything?" whispered Danny, his
eyes round and shocked.

"No!" whispered back Josh, desperately
scanning the room. He listened for buzzing or
chirping. All he could hear was Piddle the dog
barking in the yard and the far-off drone of the
vacuum cleaner. Mom was vacuuming the dining
room.

"There!" hissed Danny and pointed to the flowery duvet on Jenny's bed. Something was dancing along the yellow flowers. Something that looked confused and panicky. Of course, this thing *always* looked confused and panicky to Danny. It was a crane fly.

"A crane fly," murmured Josh. "Quick—Danny—shut the door!"

Danny got the door shut in two seconds. He bounded back to the bed to stand next to Josh and stare in wonder at their six-legged sister.

"Wow," said Danny.

"Yup," agreed Josh. "Never expected *this* to happen."

The crane fly fluttered along the flowery duvet like a nervous and not very talented dancer. It jiggled to the left and shimmied to the right and then clung to one of the cottony peaks in a shivery way.

"She must be freaking out!" marveled Danny. "What should we do?"

"Well," Josh put his head to one side and considered. "She's quite safe in here. There are no predators, probably." He looked at the quivering insect and sighed. "I suppose one of us ought to spray ourselves and go and look after her. That would be the nice thing to do."

Danny raised an eyebrow. "And since when has Jenny ever been nice to *us*?" he asked.

Josh shrugged. "She is our sister."

"Right then—off you go!" Danny handed the

S.W.I.T.C.H. spray to Josh.

"Well—can't we toss a coin or something?" said Josh.

"*You're* the one who wants to be nice!" said Danny.

Josh sighed, took the bottle and sprayed a short blast on his hand. Any part of the body seemed to do. "Just make sure you stay here and don't let Piddle in. Until we're human agai—" he said, before he too vanished.

"AARRGGH!" commented Jenny, as soon as she laid eyes on the creature frolicking toward her. Unaware that it was her little brother trying to manage more knees than could ever be right.

"I know what you mean," said Josh. "But you don't look so great, either, Jen!"

His sister's face was long, horselike, and light brown. She had two thin finger-type things poking out where her mouth should be. Two short feelers stuck up from between a pair of eyes that were large, round, bulbous, and a shimmering green-black color. Josh was still

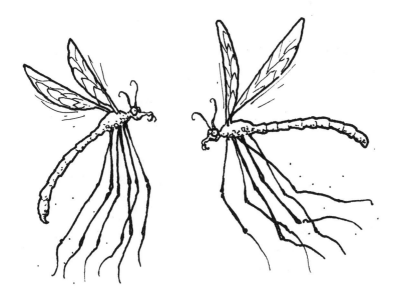

adjusting to his *own* eyes. They gave him a view as if he were looking through hundreds of tiny lenses all joined together. He'd had vision like this as an insect before. It didn't take him long to get used to the strange effect. Or to the fact that he could see almost *behind* him with these amazing eyes.

"Josh? Josh?" shrieked Jenny. She whirled around in a circle, her long, elegant brown legs staggering over the thick tufts of cotton that tangled across her duvet. Up this close, the cotton weave looked like thick woven mesh. The kind of thing you might see in a metal cable factory. "Josh?" shrieked Jenny again. "Where are you? Help me! There's a monster coming for me."

Josh sighed. "Jen-eee! I'm he-ere!" he called.

Jenny whirled her long, skinny brown body back around to face him. She screamed loudly and then fell into a crumpled heap.

"Oh do stop that!" said Josh. "Yes—I'm a crane fly! So are you! Get over it!"

"How—how—how can I be?" whimpered Jenny.

"It's a long story," said Josh. "But don't worry— it *won't last*. It's just for a short while. You'll go back to being normal at any time."

"My room's g-gone all b-big," gibbered poor Jenny. "I don't know what's going on . . ."

Josh frowned. Actually, he couldn't be sure how long Jenny's S.W.I.T.C.H.ed state would last. He and Danny had only ever had quite short, quick sprays. The effects had lasted about half an hour. The one time they had *drunk* S.W.I.T.C.H., in a special potion form, it had lasted probably ten minutes longer.

But Jenny had really sprayed a gallon of the stuff at her hair. Maybe she'd be a crane fly for *hours*.

"I—I've got six legs!" she was murmuring now. She turned around in slow circles to get a better look at her strange new body. "And wings. I can fly—sort of. Look!" And she whisked her wings into a thrumming motion.

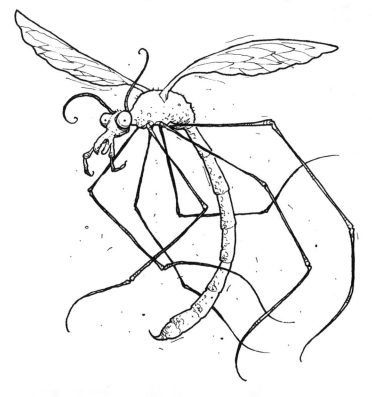

She rose up a little way above the duvet like a spindly helicopter. She wasn't very graceful. Her legs dangled about like long socks on a washing line. After a few seconds, she flopped back down on the bed. She twitched the strange brown fingery things at her mouth area and stared at Josh. "I'm dreaming, aren't I?" she said.

"Yes, that's it!" said Josh. "You are dreaming." This was *good*, he thought. Jenny really couldn't find out about the S.W.I.T.C.H. spray. Far better if she thought she was dreaming. "Yep—it's all a big weird dream," went on Josh. "Do your fishcakes wear roller skates? Mine do. Eeep."

Jenny was staring at him as if he'd gone crazy.

"It's OK—you're in a dream . . . remember?" said Josh. "Being able to fly . . . four extra legs . . . fishcakes on roller skates . . . eeep?" Nothing ever made much sense for very long in *his* dreams.

But Jenny wasn't paying attention. She had

turned away from him. She was dragging her flimsy self across the bed toward the pillow end. She walked a bit and then rose up and flapped about. Then she slumped back down for a while and then walked a little way again. It was kind of random, thought Josh. He realized, though, that he was doing the same thing. "Where are you going, Jenny?" he called after her.

"To explore my dream!" she called back. "I'm going *there*!" and she raised one of her forelegs and waved it toward a huge white edifice bathed in glowing golden light. "I've got to go there!" And now she took off and flew straight toward the glow.

"Whoa—hang on—wait!" called Josh, taking off, too, to keep up with her. He felt very wobbly in the air. This was nothing like being a housefly or a grasshopper. Those creatures had felt like well-oiled hi-tech machines. They swooped through the air and moved around like military aircraft. Being a crane fly was a lot more haphazard. The legs

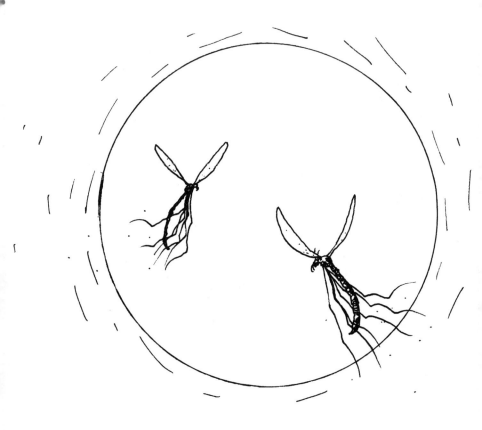

were—well—just stupid! They didn't seem
to know what to do with themselves. They
wouldn't tuck up neatly under his body. They
didn't work very well when he let them just
drop either. They swayed about and messed
up his aerodynamics.

Jenny, though, was managing to fly in spite

of her legs. She was now zooming straight toward the big golden glow. As he followed his sister, Josh felt the air around him getting warm. There was something he needed to warn Jenny about—something dangerous . . . but oh! The light! The *light*!

"Isn't it loveleeeeeee?" called back Jenny. "OW!" She suddenly jerked backward as if she'd been struck. After a confused spiral in the air, she went toward the light again. "OW!"

"Oooooooh, the pretty light!" sighed Josh, zooming toward it. "OW!" Something hot smacked him hard in the face. Dazed, he flopped onto a flat white surface, next to a huge pink spiky thing. But he didn't stay there long. "Oooooooh, the pretty light!" Once again, he was up, flying. "OW!"

"Isn't it loveleeeeeee?" sang Jenny, flapping up above him. "*OW!*"

Oooh—loveleeee! OW! Oooh—pretty—OW! It was like a strange song and dance act. He and Jenny just kept doing it. Even though they didn't know why and even though it hurt, in a bashy-burny way . . .

They were too mesmerized by the wonderful light to even notice when one of Jenny's legs fell off.

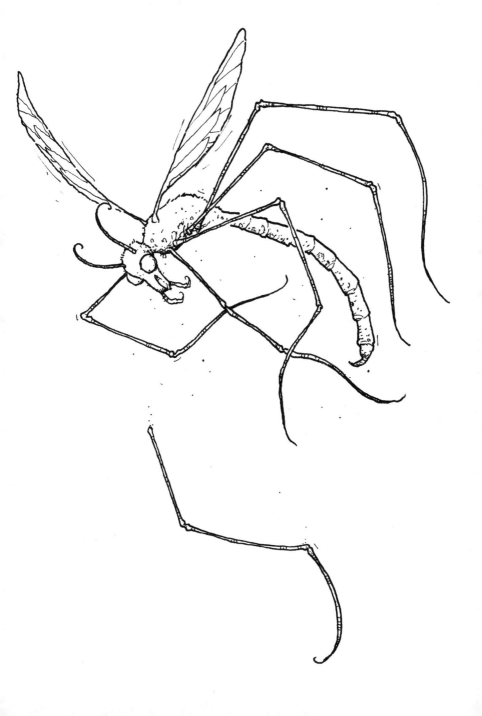

Out on a Limb

Danny had only seconds to stand gaping at his transformed brother and sister. Then Mom called out "Danny! Josh!" She began to thud slowly upstairs. The nozzle of the vacuum made sucky, thwacky noises against each of the steps as she worked her way up.

He jumped. Uh-oh! This could be a problem.

"Danny! Josh!" shouted Mom, a bit louder. "I want you to go and clean your room. Get the stuff off the carpet so I can vacuum!"

Danny gulped. He looked at the crane flies skittering about on Jenny's bed. He shuddered, even though he knew they were his brother and sister. He had to stand here and wait until they got back safely to human form. He couldn't answer Mom and be told to go and clean his room.

Mom had reached the landing now, lugging the vacuum up with her by the sound of it. She switched the vacuum cleaner off and sighed. Then she called for her sons again. And then she called for Jenny. Nobody answered. Danny stood frozen on Jenny's bedroom carpet, his heart racing. What should he do?

Mom huffed loudly outside Jenny's door and muttered to herself. "Where have they all gone? Typical, when there's work to be done."

Then she opened Jenny's door.

She looked around the room, shook her head, and sighed again. Danny stood rigid against the wall behind the door. He tried not to breathe. He'd be in big trouble if Mom found out he was hiding and not answering her. But worse, there was no way she'd let him stay in Jenny's room, guarding a couple of crane flies.

Mom's fingers curled around the edge of the door. She huffed again. And then—mercifully—the door was pulled closed.

Danny sprang toward the bed. He couldn't see the crane flies now. But a buzzy clicking noise told him they were flying against something. Ah! There they were, flapping around the lamp on Jenny's white-painted bedside table.

"Ooh, that's got to hurt," winced Danny. He watched them ping against the hot bulb and do backflips away from it. They rebounded off the inside of the cone-shaped lampshade. "Josh!" he hissed, aware that Mom was still up on the landing. "Don't be an idiot. Stop head-butting the light!"

But they kept doing it. Again and again, even though it was clearly hurting them. Danny was about to reach out and switch the lamp off when he saw something shocking on the bedside table, next to Jenny's pink hairbrush. He hoped it was a funny shaped hair—but it was too dark. Jenny's hairs were blonde. This was dark colored and looked very much like . . .

"A leg!" gasped Danny. "One of them's lost a leg!"

"Stop! Jenny! Stop!" puffed Josh, lying in a bedraggled heap on her bedside table. "Look! You've lost a leg!"

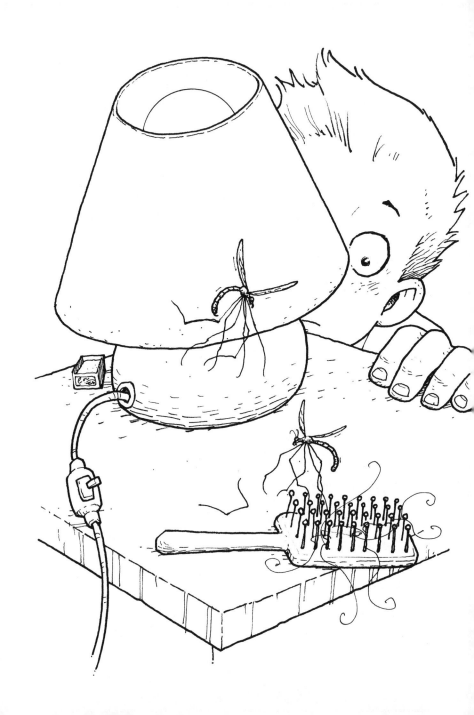

He knew it wasn't his leg, as he'd just done a quick check and he still had all six. Jenny, though, had only five. One of her back legs was missing. And here it was, lying next to the big pink spiky thing that Josh had figured out was Jenny's hairbrush. He might not ever have noticed the leg if he hadn't got so exhausted. It was only because he *couldn't* fly at the light now that he had stopped. And resting had given him a moment to realize that he and his sister had gone nuts, just like the moth she'd tried to kill earlier. They had all thought the light was the moon and were instinctively trying to fly toward it to safety. But in fact, it was the bulb in the bedside lamp. Josh's head and feet were very sore with all the burns from smacking against the white-hot glass.

Jenny suddenly slapped down next to him, groaning. "What?" she said. "What did you say?"

"Look—I don't want you to get upset," began Josh.

"About what? Hurry up—I've got to fly to the light!" She was pulling herself up again already. "The lovely light!"

"STOP!" yelled Josh. "Can't you see that's your bedside lamp? You're just banging yourself against a white-hot bit of glass!"

"What?" said Jenny, again. She had flopped down beside him once more.

"And look—you've lost a leg," said Josh. He waved one of his own legs at the poor specimen lying by the hairbrush.

"Ooh," said Jenny, checking her limbs and noting the stump at the back. "I thought something stung a bit." She peered at the useless limb.

"Ah well," said Josh. "You've got some more."

But he gulped. Would he switch back and discover Jenny had lost an arm or a leg for good. Why did crane flies have to be so *flimsy*?

At this moment, Danny was reaching toward the bedside lamp. He was carefully avoiding the collapsed crane flies below it, trying to switch off the tormenting, dangerous light before any more legs fell off. Before he'd reached the switch, the bedroom door, which Mom hadn't completely shut, was suddenly knocked open. In trotted Piddle.

Piddle, a small terrier dog (called Piddle because of an unattractive habit he had when he got overexcited) was very pleased to see Danny. He was bored and wanted to play. He yapped and jumped up on Jenny's bed, even though he wasn't allowed to.

"Piddle! Get out!" hissed Danny. He couldn't shout. Mom was in the bathroom now and might hear him. But Piddle could see that Danny was playing with something. He was pointing his hand at the bedside table. What was going on?

"*OUT!*" hissed Danny, as loudly as he dared. Piddle heard him. But what he decided Danny was actually saying was "*LOOK! LOOK! TAKE A LOOK AT THIS!*"

"It's not good, is it?" said Jenny, booting her detached leg about with one of her attached ones. "I should be bleeding to death."

"Nah—you're all right," gulped Josh. He tried hard not to think of switching back to Stumpsville. "Crane flies lose legs like you lose a fingernail. It's a survival thing. If they get caught by a predator, they can just shake a leg off and escape."

"Ugh," said Jenny. She examined the stump where her leg had been. It wasn't oozing anything at all. She looked up at the light and sighed longingly.

"NO-OO!" warned Josh. "Don't fly to the light! You know it doesn't make sense!"

"But . . ." sighed Jenny. Then she snapped her head around to Josh and said, "Hang on—predator? You said predator! Are there predators in my dream? I hate dreams like that. I'm going to have to wake myself up if there's a predator after me."

"We should be OK," said Josh. "We're in your bedroom. I don't think there are any big predators there except you. And you're not around."

Jenny nodded and then froze. Her big bulbous eyes seemed to get even bigger and more bulbous. A very loud gusty noise suddenly burst into their ears. Jenny stared in horror at something behind Josh. Josh spun around, his legs flapping, and stared too. A huge shadowy figure loomed high into the air. That was probably Danny, Josh told himself. What was far more terrifying was the smaller but still pretty enormous creature. It was suddenly springing up and down in front of the bedside table.

A blast of warm air, which smelled of rotten old meat, suddenly sent Josh and Jenny flying back toward the big yellow base of the lamp. Jenny screamed. Fair enough, thought Josh, and joined her. "AAARGH!" they agreed, as a pair of jaws the size of a tractor snapped shut inches away from them. Another blast of nasty warm, meaty air blew at them.

"OH NO!" shrieked Josh. "It's PIDDLE!" He stared at Jenny in horror. "Piddle EATS creepy-crawlies!"

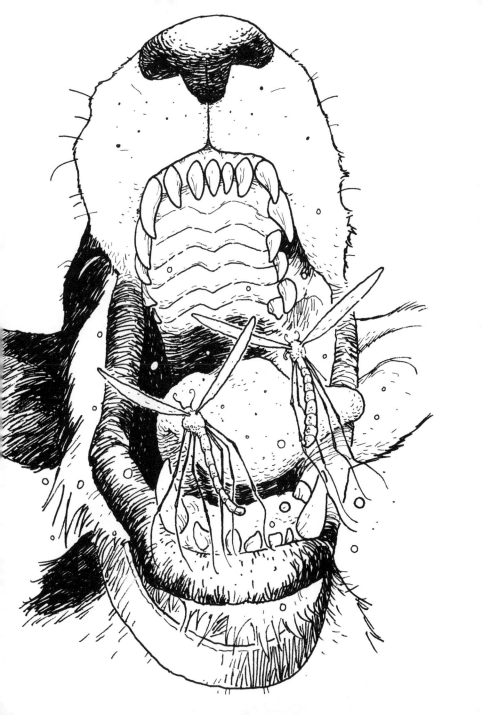

Fetch!

With his front legs, Josh grabbed hold of Jenny by the wings. He dragged her around to the back of the lampshade. They huddled together on a large plastic tray filled with blue glitter. "Ooh," said Jenny. "I wondered where my eye shadow had gone . . ."

"Jenny!" squawked Josh. "Don't you think there are more important things to worry about right now? We're about to be eaten by a giant Piddle!" He cringed back into the corner as a hairy white paw with thick yellow claws suddenly whacked across the table top to their left with a scrunch. It scratched four grooves in the paint. A terrible shrill sound ripped through the air, like a train crashing very fast over and over again. Piddle was yapping. The looming shadow that must be Danny was swooping down on top of Piddle. Would he manage to stop the energetic terrier in time?

"We won't be eaten by Piddle," said Jenny, quite calmly, even though she was shaking as much as Josh.

"What? How do you know *that*?" gasped Josh. He dragged them both farther backward as a smelly pink tongue suddenly shot around the edge of the lamp.

"Because it's *my* dream," said Jenny, shrugging with all five of her legs. "And in my dreams, whenever I'm being chased by a monster, it never *actually* gets me. I always wake up just before that happens."

"B-but . . . " Josh couldn't think of an answer to this. Telling Jenny this was all real probably wouldn't help much.

"Of course *you* might get eaten," went on Jenny, with a cheerful chuckle. "You quite often do get eaten or squashed or thrown off a cliff or something, in my dreams. Although Danny is *usually* the first one to bite the dust. But not me. Nope. In fact, I've had enough of this dream now." Jenny struggled to stand up straight again.

"I'm just going around to face the monster and then I'll wake up."

"JENNY! NO!" yelled Josh, horrified, trying to grab her. "YOU CAN'T! PIDDLE WILL EAT YOU!"

"No, he won't—you'll see," said Jenny. She fluttered up above him. Then she scooted around to the front of the lamp again.

"Eww!" she said, as she noticed her discarded leg being licked up by a tongue the size of the kitchen table. The leg disappeared as a shaggy white mouth snapped shut.

"Come on then!" yelled Jenny, bobbing up and down in front of the most terrifying sight she had ever seen (but just not believing it). "Have another one!"

And she yanked off another leg and threw it in Piddle's face. "FETCH!" she shouted.

Josh scuttled around the lamp and hid behind the hairbrush. "JENNY!" he wailed. "STOP IT! You're going to get EATEN!"

The snappy, yappy jaws were back, wide open. The tongue was quivering up and down between sharp, yellowy canine teeth. Jenny watched her second leg sail in and the jaws snap shut. Now she had only four legs left. She stood, laughing and bobbing up and down, in the face of doom. She looked a bit like a foldout camping table.

"You want another piece of me?" she yelled. "See if I care!"

She looked around and was trying to decide which leg to pull off next. Josh made a run for it. He grabbed her around her spindly middle and began to drag her away. "STOP pulling your legs off!" he gasped as she flapped around, angrily. His wings went into overdrive. He managed to drag her up into the air before she could turn herself into a tripod.

"This is *my* dream!" snapped Jenny, struggling hard. "And I'll pull as many legs off as I want! Get out of my dream! You're always coming in and messing with my stuff. I'm telling Mom! Get—"

"—OFF!" yelped Danny and grabbed Piddle by the collar. He yanked the dog away from the bedside table. He couldn't see any insect life there at all. He stared, horrified, into the terrier's mouth. Piddle was panting excitedly, his tail wagging. His

tongue was lolloping about between his sharp
teeth. And on the tongue were a couple of legs.
Crane fly legs. "*Oh no*," whimpered Danny. "Josh!
Jenny! *Noo!*"

Then a movement caught his eye. He saw a
bundle of legs and wings floundering up the wall
toward the window. Two crane flies! There were
still *two*! The leg count didn't look great for one of
them, but they were still alive!

Danny bundled Piddle out of the room. He shut the door fast. He lay back against it, his heart thumping in his chest. He'd had such a scare. He'd really thought his dog had just eaten half his family. As he watched Josh and Jenny fluttering along the windowsill, he started to calm down again. He would just sit here, nice and calm, until they popped back up as humans again. That's all. Nothing else.

"Josh? Danny? Jenny? Are you in there?" called Mom from down in the bathroom. Oh no! She must have heard him shut the door after he'd chucked Piddle out. If she came in now, he would never be able to stay and protect Josh and Jenny. Especially if they started that idiotic lightbulb-butting thing again.

Danny looked around him in a panic as Mom switched off the vacuum. She stepped out onto the landing. She was heading back to look in Jenny's room again. This time she was suspicious, so she was *sure* to look behind the door.

She would haul him out, tell him off, and send him to his room. And then anything might happen to Jenny and Josh! Danny gulped as he heard Mom walk across the landing toward Jenny's door. Maybe he should just tell her everything and hope she would believe him and . . . "Oh come *on*!" he said to himself. Then he grabbed the S.W.I.T.C.H. spray. He dove down behind the bed and squirted a yellow blast of it at his head.

The In Crowd

Danny had only just enough time to shove the spray bottle under Jenny's bed before it shot up to the size of a telephone booth. The walls and ceiling of Jenny's room rushed away from him, stretching out to the size of a football stadium.

He knew, of course, that nothing had gotten bigger at all. It was just he—along with Josh and Jenny—who'd gotten suddenly a lot smaller. Danny stood up carefully, trying to sort out his weird eyes. It was that funny multi-lens thing again. A bit like looking through one of those glass things that gave you tons of the same view in many tiny hexagons. After a few seconds, though, he got used to it. His vision seemed quite normal. He tested out his legs. At least this time—for once—he had *known* what he was going to turn into before he got sprayed. He tried out his wings. He soon found himself rising up beside the vast football field-sized bed, in a rather wobbly way.

It was nowhere near as good as being a housefly or a grasshopper. Now, *those* things knew how to move! Still, it would have to do.

There was a sudden breeze. Danny whirled around to see the door opening and the humongous silhouette of what must be his mom. He'd only just sprayed himself in time! Over on the windowsill, which now looked like a very wide flat runway on the edge of a cliff, Danny could see Josh and Jenny. They were clinging to the windowpane and bobbing up and down in that nervous crane fly way.

"How are you doing?" he asked, casually, landing behind them. He glanced back into the room but couldn't see Mom now. Maybe she'd gone back out onto the landing

"Danny! What are *you* doing here?" asked Jenny. "It's bad enough having *one* annoying little brother in my dream, let alone two! I don't get any peace, even while I'm asleep!"

"Hey!" protested Josh, flickering his funny fingery mouthparts. "I just saved your life!"

"No, you didn't!" argued Jenny. "You just had to interfere! I was going to wake up, if you hadn't come along. But now I'm still in this stupid dream, thanks to you. And now it looks like—" she glared at Danny "—it's just gotten a lot stupider!"

"Dream?" muttered Danny, fluttering closer to Josh.

"Yep. That's what she thinks this is," Josh muttered back. "She just pulled her own leg off! She doesn't think it's anything to worry about . . ."

"Ah," said Danny.

"What are you doing here?" said Josh. "You're supposed to be guarding us until we get back to normal. And you're not doing a great job of it, are you? Piddle nearly ate us!"

"I know. I'm sorry," said Danny. "I shut the door. But then Mom came in looking for us. I had to hide. Then she didn't shut the door properly, and so Piddle got in. I stopped him! I put him outside again."

"And you're here now—because?" snapped Josh.

"Because she came in again. I had to shrink down and hide, or she'd make me go out. I couldn't guard you then, could I?"

Josh batted his feelers together wearily. "OK. How do you think you can guard us now, Danny? Now that *you* need guarding too!"

"Oh," said Danny. "I never thought of that."

"Ah well," sighed Josh as Jenny fluttered up and down the windowpane, singing a little song. "It can't last much longer, anyway. Jenny's got to change back soon. Then I will—and I'll have to guard you until you do. So we must stay safely on the windowsill until then. I just hope the light thing doesn't start up again." He stared wistfully at the golden glow beside the bed. Danny looked

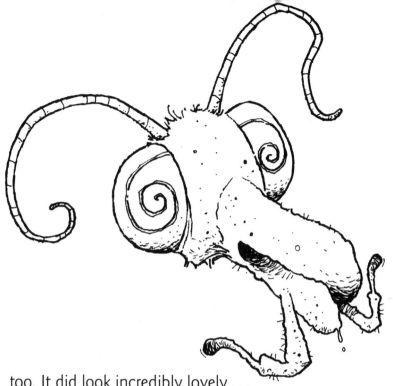

too. It did look incredibly lovely . . .

"NO!" said Josh, grabbing Danny's wings before he could take off. "There's nothing for you there. Except a burnt face!"

Josh and Danny joined Jenny. They scuttled up and down the windowpane, staring through the thick glass, out into the garden. It was almost dark, and the streetlights were coming on. *They* looked nice too . . . apart from the tickle-tickle-tickle noises of their feet on the glass, it was all quite peaceful.

"Oh look! It's Chelsea and Louise!" Jenny suddenly squeaked. "Hey! Chelsea! Lou!"

Outside they could see two of Jenny's friends walking along the street toward the house, chatting together. "Chelsea! Lou!" shouted Jenny, excitedly. "Up here!" And she flapped her pathetic legs against the glass.

"Umm . . . Jen," said Josh. "I don't think they can hear you!"

Suddenly, with a vroom of her spindly wings, Jenny shot up the windowpane. Josh and Danny realized, to their horror, that she was heading for a narrow gap where one of the small top windows was ajar.

"Jenny! NO! Don't go out!" yelled Danny. But it was no good. Jenny wasn't listening. She was already mostly outside, one last leg flicking through after her.

"Now what?" gasped Josh. "How did *that* happen? We're supposed to be keeping her safe!"

"Quick! After her," yelled Danny. He hurtled up the glass and through the gap after his sister.

The cool evening air was quite refreshing as

Danny and Josh drifted through it, trying to see where Jenny had gone. It smelled of damp grass and late summer blossom. Moths and midges zoomed around them, thrumming and whining.

"There!" said Josh. "She's down there! Oh no! What does she think she's doing?"

Jenny had always been popular with the girls at school. Somehow, tonight, they weren't so interested. As she glided toward them, calling out their names, the girls at first ignored her. This wasn't so bad.

"It's OK—they're ignoring her," said Josh. He chuckled. "She won't like that!"

"Noooo," said Danny flapping along beside him. He dodged a rather heavyweight moth that was giving him a funny look as it bumbled past. "Her best friends ignoring her won't do her any harm. It's the bit when they try to kill her that is going to upset her."

He wasn't wrong. Four seconds later, Jenny fluttered eagerly in front of Chelsea's nose. A lot of shrieking split the evening air. Both Chelsea and Louise began to bash frantically at the creepy leggy thing in their faces.

"UGGH! KILL IT! KILL IT! GET IT OFF ME!"
squealed Chelsea.

Poor Jenny did somersaults through the air,
horrified. Josh and Danny swooped down and
managed to catch her. "Stop!" yelled Danny. Josh
restrained his sister from going back for another
try. "Don't bother, Jen! They're not worth it!"

"I never liked them anyway," added Josh.

Jenny sniffed. "I thought they were my *friends*."

"Yes, but that was before you turned into a four-
legged freak," pointed out Danny.

"And remember," added Josh. "This is just a
dream, anyway."

"Ooooooh!" said Jenny. She began to flap her
way toward something new. She flapped so hard
she dragged Josh and Danny with her.

This time it was an *orange* light. A bulb in
an orange glass shade, which hung from the
wooden beam above a front porch. It was a bit of
a jumping, jiving hot spot. It was already heaving
with the local nightlife. Three large moths were
spiraling around inside it. At least a dozen midges
were bouncing up and down in the cooler pool

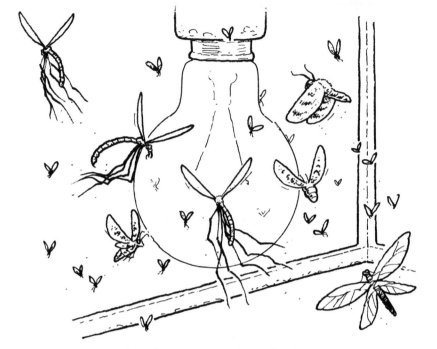

of light by the glass rim. A dozy-looking, see-through lacewing swayed about in one corner, gazing into a dazzling crystal cube up by the hot metal bulb socket.

"Oh not *this* again!" moaned Josh as he and Danny were dragged in with Jenny. "Jen! You know you'll only end up getting hurt!"

But Jenny was already head-butting the porch light. Danny was right up there next to her. Their cries of delight and pain echoed all around the orange glass room created by the outdoor lightshade.

Josh shivered and made himself turn away
from the light. The glow was so incredibly
tempting! He peered out into the night sky and
saw something black and arrow-shaped suddenly
zoom past. It made him
gulp with horror. He
knew what that was. He
had seen it circling their
garden on many warm
summer evenings. It was a
bat. A pipistrelle bat. And
pipistrelles liked nothing
better than a mouthful of
crane fly.

Josh took a deep breath and turned around.
Ignoring the dozy green lacewing as it fluttered
past him into the night air, he dived back into the
orange insect disco. He managed to tangle his
limbs around Danny and Jenny and tug them back
outside. "There!" he said, pointing a leg at Jenny's
bedroom window. "That's the light we want! That
one!" And he zoomed straight for it, dragging his
siblings with him.

The dark arrow flitted by so close that he heard himself scream. Then he realized it wasn't his scream. The dozy-looking lacewing shot over his head, feebly flapping in the vicious teeth of the bat.

Thud-thud-thud. They hit the bedroom window. Then Josh dragged Jenny and Danny up to the opening and shoved them through it. Exhausted, they all slid down the inside of the glass and landed in a quivering heap on the sill.

For a few seconds there was peace.

Until . . .

VROOOOOOOOOOOOOOOOOOOOOOOOOOO OOOOOOOOO

"What is THAT?" screamed Jenny.

This Sucks

Josh and Danny stared at each other, mystified. They had heard some weird noises when they'd been shrunk down to creepy-crawlies before but nothing like this. The howling, droning noise just went on and on. And it was getting louder.

"Uh-oh!" gulped Danny, as a gigantic figure loomed back into Jenny's bedroom. It was all too big to take in properly. He could see a long shining thing, moving in front of the gigantic figure. The long shining thing was making the VROOOOOOOO noise. It was moving from side to side. And getting closer.

"What *is* it?" asked Josh. Jenny squeaked and shut her wings up tight and scrunched her four legs close together.

"It's Mom," said Danny. "And the vacuum."

"Oh dear," said Josh.

"Oh help!" yelled Danny. "It's coming this way." And it was. The long shiny thing was waving through the air. Mom always vacuumed the cobwebs off the wall, ceilings, and . . . windowsills!

CRASH!

Suddenly the shiny metal tube, with an enormous round, black sucking mouth, was at the far end of the windowsill. A cloud of dust and cobwebs was swirling up in front of it and then being whipped away into the dark tunnel. A tunnel from which there could be no escape.

"FLY! FLY!" shrieked Danny. They all shimmied up into the air, shrieking with fear. The sucking nozzle swept along the sill to the corner where they'd been crouched seconds earlier. Then it began to climb up toward the top corner of the window. The three crane flies were flapping about in a kind of multi-legged disco dance of terror.

"Outside again!" yelled Danny. But Josh saw the black arrow shape flicker past, seeking more insect munchies.

"NO—THIS WAY!" bawled Josh. He shot across the glass at an angle, past the upper end of the nozzle. He dropped down as fast as he could go, off the edge of the sill and into a dark narrow chasm.

Plop! Plop! Jenny and Danny skidded in behind him. They all clung to the dusty wallpaper, jiggling up and down with shock. "We should be safe here," whispered Josh. "We're down behind the radiator."

"What about spiders?" said Danny, looking around edgily. He'd come horribly close to getting eaten by a spider when he spent some time being a housefly earlier that summer.

"Can't see any," said Josh.

"OK—what about when she changes back?" said Danny. "It can't be long now before she cha— I mean, before she *wakes up from her dream*," he added, realizing that Jenny was listening. "She's going to end up a bit flat!"

Josh nodded. Changing back to normal would be impossible behind the radiator. Jenny would get squished. She would look like a human waffle.

"Look—I don't know what I'm doing here," said Jenny, suddenly. "This is a stupid dream, and I've had enough of it. I'm going to meet the sucky monster and get it over with. Then I'll wake up."

"No! Jenny—don't!" yelled Danny and Josh.

She looked quite surprised. "You *don't* want me to get sucked up by a monster? Man, that's a shock. Well, in that case, I'll just have to wake myself up!" She scrunched up her horsey brown face. The little fingery bits on her mouth twiddled through the air as she concentrated hard.

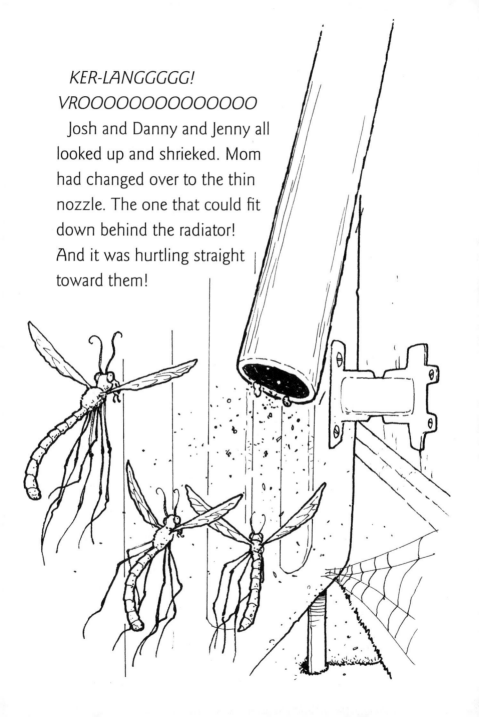

KER-LANGGGGG!
VROOOOOOOOOOOOOOO

Josh and Danny and Jenny all looked up and shrieked. Mom had changed over to the thin nozzle. The one that could fit down behind the radiator! And it was hurtling straight toward them!

Nozzly Nightmare

Danny went first. He was the closest. He suddenly found his wings were being dragged upward by the sucking vortex of air that was funneling up into the nozzle. The end of the nozzle was flattened and narrow. But it was still wide enough to suck him right through.

"HEEELP!" he yelled as he tried to hang on to one of the fixings that held the radiator to the wall. First, his back legs flew up behind him . . . then the middle ones . . . then . . . "AAARGH!" he screamed as he lost his grip and shot up through the air, spinning and twisting.

"DANEEEE!" shouted Josh, trying vainly to catch him as he was flung past.

"DANEEEE!" cried Jenny. And she lost her grip too and was whipped away up after her little brother.

"NO! JENNY! DANNY! COME BACK!" wailed Josh, even as his own back legs were pulled off the wall. He was tugged up, up, to the swirling black funnel of death. He could just imagine spinning and flailing all the way up the metal nozzle. Along the wobbly plastic tube into the big chamber full of dust and fluff and old chips and dried-up peas and toenails and dead flies and dead spiders and dead . . . he gulped . . . crane flies. It was a vacuum tomb. And he was going into it . . .

THWIP! Up he shot, and he had only time to notice the black rim of the nozzle whacking his legs together

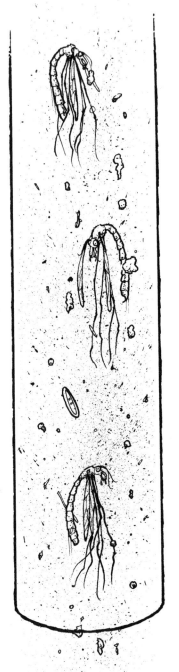

when all of a sudden there was a *CLUNK*. And the *VROOOOOO* noise went *VROOo-oo-o-sssssssssssssss*. And stopped.

Josh clung on to the rim of the narrow nozzle, staring around in amazement. Someone had switched the vacuum off! It was OFF.

Then, in the silence, he heard a whimper. He turned, peering up into the dusty gloom of the nozzle tube. He could just make out a tangle of skinny brown limbs and wings and four eyes a little way above him.

"Danny? Jenny?! Are you OK?" he squeaked. They squeaked back. And then they wriggled, and a second later, they were tumbling down to him. All three of them fell out of the nozzle in a leggy knot and hurtled down to the floor. They didn't have much time to get any of their wings going, but fortunately it was a soft landing. They fell on one of Jenny's slippers.

For a moment they just stared at one another. Then they began the job of untangling and counting limbs. Jenny was sniffing a bit. "You tried to save me," she murmured. "You know, even though it's just a dream, that was quite sweet of you both . . . "

Danny and Josh stared at her for a few astonished moments. Then they shook their heads and carried on with the leg sorting.

"How many legs have you lost?" said Danny.

"Two," said Josh. "You?"

"One. And a half," said Danny, inspecting the one that was snapped off at the knee. "It does sting a bit, doesn't it?"

"How about you, Jenny?" asked Josh.

"I feel funny," said Jenny. She had only three legs left. Her wings were all scrunched up. There was something about the look on her face that warned Josh and Danny to back away. Fast.

"Here she goes!" yelled Josh. "Fly for it! NOOOW!"

Mom unplugged the vacuum and then wound up the cord. There was a thud. She turned around. She stared in astonishment at her daughter, who was lying down next to the radiator, waving her legs in the air and going, "One—two! One—two! I've got two legs! Two legs! Not three! Phew!"

"How did you get down there?" Mom asked, mystified. She didn't notice two crane flies that flapped past her left ear and out onto the landing.

"I don't know," said Jenny, scratching her head. "I think I've been working too hard at school. I just had the freakiest dream . . ."

Seeing the Light

Mom looked into Danny and Josh's room. "Oh! So you're back now, Josh. Where's Danny?"

Josh turned around, with his hands cupped together. "Oh—he's around," he smiled, brightly. He seemed quite out of breath.

"What have you got there?" asked Mom, warily. She knew how much Josh loved creepy-crawlies.

"Oh—just a little friend," said Josh. He opened his fingers to reveal a crane fly with only four and a half limbs.

"He's been through the wars!" said Mom, squinting at Danny.

"Mmmm," said Josh, giving her a rather hard stare.

As Mom went outside again, she heard another thud and grinned, shaking her head. Danny must have been hiding! The boys were playing one of their games.

Danny and Josh ran into Jenny's room.

"Get OUT of my—" began Jenny, but they ignored her. They dug under the bed and retrieved the S.W.I.T.C.H. spray.

"This is our bottle," said Josh. "We put water and . . . and . . ."

". . . Piddle's piddle in it!" added Danny.

"Oooh—you disgusting little . . ." Jenny trailed off. She was staring at her bedside lamp in a dreamy way. Josh ran to put the S.W.I.T.C.H. spray up at the farthest corner of the top shelf of their highest cupboard.

DING-DONG! chimed the front door. "Jenny!" called up Mom. "It's Chelsea and Louise!"

Danny and Josh sat at the top of the stairs and watched Jenny walk down. Chelsea and Louise stood by the door. "Hi!" they both called. "You want to come out?"

Jenny stared at them through narrow eyes, her arms folded.

"Come on," laughed Chelsea. "What are you looking all funny about? You wait till you hear what we've heard about Kelly Smith! You'll just *die!*"

"Yes. I might just do that," snapped Jenny. "You know . . . I don't think I do want to come out with you tonight. The pair of you—you just *kill* me!"

Chelsea and Louise stared at Jenny and then at each other, as she propelled them back outside.

"OK—don't get in a flap, Jen," giggled Chelsea. "Come on out! Just as you are. You look great in that short skirt. All leggy!"

Jenny stared at her legs and then glared at Chelsea. "Just don't feel like going out tonight," she growled.

"So—what—you're just going to sit at home all evening?" gasped Louise, astonished.

"Yes," said Jenny. "I'll see you tomorrow. But tonight, for some reason, I just want to look at my bedside lamp."

She didn't even notice Josh and Danny rolling about laughing on the landing as she stomped back upstairs.

Shady Secret

"Here! Take it back!" said Danny, as soon as Petty opened her front door. He thrust the spray bottle into her hand. She scowled and pulled them quickly into her hallway, slamming the door shut behind them.

"Have you forgotten *everything* I've told you?" she demanded. "Remember—we may be being watched! At any time! I told you, there are government spies always keeping me under surveillance."

Josh folded his arms. "But if this Victor Crouch guy *really* burnt out your memory and got you kicked out of the government's secret science labs, why would they bother with you again? They must think you don't know anything."

"You really don't pay attention, do you?" snapped Petty. "Victor Crouch realized—too late—that the research he stole from me was fake! He will not have been able to make S.W.I.T.C.H. spray himself. The code for making it is here, with me! And all *he* got was the *fake* code.

"So he will be having me watched, just in case I look like I might be able to remember again. He's hoping I'll still be active."

"Active?" echoed Danny.

"Yesss! Working as a genius scientist once more. Which, of course, I am! But nobody knows it except me and you. So that's why we have to be careful. I have to carry on looking like a scatterbrained old biddy. And *you* have to carry on looking for the missing REPTOSWITCH cubes, if we're ever going to make the reptile spray. I don't suppose you've found another one, have you?"

Petty wandered into her kitchen and took two small velvet boxes off a high shelf. She opened the red one to reveal six sparkling glass cubes, each with a tiny hologram inside it. These were BUGSWITCH cubes, each containing a vital part of the code for making BUGSWITCH spray.

Petty smiled and ran her fingertips over the six cubes. Then she opened the green velvet box, revealing only four cubes in a tray meant for six.

There had been only one cube when Josh and Danny first saw the box. They had managed to find three of the missing ones. "I tried to figure out the code with just these four cubes last week," Petty said. "I thought I might be able to remember the missing parts. But I can't. If you two can't find the last two cubes, I might as well give up."

"Well, we are trying, you know," said Danny. "When we're not having to deal with the trouble your S.W.I.T.C.H. spray keeps making for us! Did you know that our sister was S.W.I.T.C.H.ed on Wednesday?!"

Petty dropped onto a kitchen chair, shocked. "No!"

Josh and Danny told her what had happened. "But you don't have to worry," said Josh, at the end of their story. "She thinks it was all a dream."

Petty sighed and took her glasses off. "I think I'm going to have to lie down under a damp towel," she said. "Come on. Better go home now, boys. Sorry about your sister."

As she shooed them onto the front step, Danny glanced up. "Hey!" he said. "That was the little orange room we flew into! We were up in there, head-butting your light!"

They all stared up into the porch lightshade. Then Josh squinted. "Wait a minute," he said. "Petty—can you get me a chair?"

"Whatever for?" snapped Petty.

"I remember seeing something up in that

light . . . something strange . . ." Josh screwed up his eyes. Yes . . . there was a strange little sparkle of light up inside the glass shade.

Petty brought out a chair. Josh stood on it. Reaching up, on his tiptoes, he put his hand into the shade. Two dead moths fell out. Danny gave a little shriek. "Well . . ." he said. "I met them a couple of nights ago!"

Josh stepped back off the chair with something in his hand. He smiled at Petty and opened his fingers. In his palm lay a glass cube, with the hologram of a gecko inside it.

"REPTOSWITCH cube, anyone?" said Josh.

Top Secret!

For Petty Potts's Eyes Only!!

DIARY ENTRY *612.3

SUBJECT: FIVE REPTILE SWITCH CUBES!!!

Hurrah! Getting Josh and Danny into the project paid off again today. They had another S.W.I.T.C.H. adventure and ended up in my porch light. Where it turns out I had hidden the fifth REPTOSWITCH cube!

It is a bit worrying that their sister got caught up in things and was also turned into a crane fly. But both boys insist that she still thinks it was only some kind of weird dream.

Another worry are the flashes of light. I have seen them several times now. In the trees at the park and in the hedges opposite my house. I was certain I saw a flash when Josh got up on the chair and pulled the REPTOSWITCH cube out of the porch light.

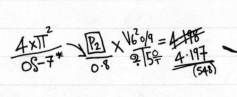

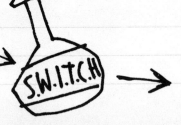

It could just be an old broken bottle reflecting the sun. Or it could be someone spying on me through binoculars. Victor Crouch's spies could be anywhere! I keep imagining that old eyebrow-less freak staring through my windows . . .

But I suppose I do have to remember that sometimes I see and hear things that aren't really there. That's all part of the package when you're a genius. I will make sure Josh and Danny keep very watchful, though.

Just in case.

But when we find the last cube, I can start trying out REPTOSWITCH spray on them! And if I can persuade them to be an alligator for an hour or two, perhaps I can also persuade them to snack on Victor Crouch!!!

Ah ha! Ah ha-ha-ha-ha! Umm. Scary powerful laugh, etc. (It doesn't really work, written down, does it?)

<u>REMEMBER</u>

Recommended Reading

BOOKS
Want to brush up on your bug knowledge? Here's a list of books dedicated to creepy-crawlies.

Glaser, Linda. *Not a Buzz to Be Found.* Minneapolis: Millbrook Press, 2012.

Heos, Bridget. *What to Expect When You're Expecting Larvae: A Guide for Insect Parents (and Curious Kids).* Minneapolis: Millbrook Press, 2011.

Markle, Sandra. Insect World series. Minneapolis: Lerner Publications, 2008.

WEBSITES
Find out more about nature and wildlife using the websites below.

BioKids
http://www.biokids.umich.edu/critters/
The University of Michigan's Critter Catalog has

a ton of pictures of different kinds of bugs and information on where they live, how they behave, and their predators.

National Geographic Kids

http://video.nationalgeographic.com/video/kids/animals-pets-kids/bugs-kids

Go to this fun website to watch clips from National Geographic about all sorts of creepy-crawlies.

U.S. Fish & Wildlife Service

http://www.fws.gov/letsgooutside/kids.html

This website has lots of activities for when you're outside playing and looking for wildlife.

CHECK OUT ALL OF THE

#1 Spider Stampede

Eight-year-olds Josh and Danny discover that their neighbor Miss Potts has a secret formula that can change people into bugs. Soon enough, they find themselves with six extra legs. Can the boys survive in the world as spiders long enough to make it home in time for dinner?

#2 Fly Frenzy

Danny and Josh are avoiding their neighbor because she "accidentally" turned them into bugs. But when their mom's garden is ruined the day before a big competition, the twins turn into bluebottle houseflies to discover the culprits. Will they find who's responsible before it's too late?

#3 Grasshopper Glitch

Danny and Josh are having a normal day at school . . . until they turn into grasshoppers in the middle of class! Can they avoid being eaten during their whirlwind search to find the antidote? And will they be able to change back before getting a week of detention?